Baiting Hollow: A Time of Enchantment

By

Patricia Clark Smith

Order this book online at www.trafford.com
or email orders@trafford.com

Most Trafford titles are also available at major online book retailers.

Note for Librarians: A cataloguing record for this book is available from Library
and Archives Canada at www.collectionscanada.ca/amicus/index-e.html

Printed in Victoria, BC, Canada.

ISBN: 978-1-4269-1822-3 (sc)

Library of Congress Control Number: 2009937364

*Our mission is to efficiently provide the world's finest, most
comprehensive book publishing service, enabling every author to
experience success. To find out how to publish your book, your way, and
have it available worldwide, visit us online at www.trafford.com*

Trafford rev. 11/16/09

www.trafford.com

North America & international
toll-free: 1 888 232 4444 (USA & Canada)
phone: 250 383 6864 ♦ fax: 812 355 4082

Baiting Hollow: A Time of Enchantment

Dedicated with love to my mersister,
Barbara,
my inspiration, my guide, my muse,
for her faith, love, encouragement,
and imagination.
Thank you!

Although El Nino had wrecked havoc on the west coast, Connecticut had enjoyed a mild winter. It was the end of March and all around Brigit's Connecticut home the purple crocus were blooming, the yellow daffodils were about to open, and the pink tulips were just peaking out of the warm spring soil in her mother's garden.

Brigit loved to walk outside with her morning orange juice to see what surprises, what wonders the garden had in store. Everything was perfect for the advent of the spring flower show. Her family's raking, weeding, and edging last weekend had really paid off. The garden was clean, neat, and coming alive. What a joy it was to see the early spring flowers in bloom, and the day lilies, sweet william, and pinks poke through the ground.

Brigit walked around back to the small strawberry patch her father cleared for her last summer. Uncle David had given her two dozen small strawberry plants from the Twomey farm on Long Island, and her mother showed her how to plant them in neat and tidy rows.

Last summer Uncle David told her the strawberry plants would have tiny white blossoms which would produce fruit,

but for the first growing season it was
important to pinch off the white flowers.
If the little plants were not allowed to
produce fruit the first summer, the plants'
energy would go into the plants' growth.
Uncle David promised that if Brigit followed
his directions, her plants would triple in
size and have triple the crop the second
year. "Patience is one key to growing
strawberries," Uncle David said. Brigit
stooped down and touched a strawberry
leaf. The early morning dew on the leaf
looked like silver tear drops. A soft breeze,
the morning sunlight, robins' chirping, and
beautiful flowers surrounded her. Winter

Patricia Clark Smith.

was over. In three months her strawberries would be ready for harvest.

Walking back to the house, Brigit remembered picking strawberries with her sister, Barbara, and Aunt Mame at the Twomey farm. Now, she was imagining quarts of strawberries from her own strawberry patch. She imagined picking, washing, cutting, and mashing them while her mother made Aunt Mame's shortcake recipe. Brigit could almost taste strawberry shortcake with real cream on top. "Mmm," she hummed. "I think imagination is another key to growing strawberries."

The garage door opened and distracted Brigit from her sweet daydream. Her sister, Maggie, was pulling the car out of the garage. Brigit walked to the side of the driveway as the car slowly backed out. Maggie was sixteen years old and had a part time job at the local Five and Dime store. During her junior year at Farmington High School she was elected class secretary and was a member of the National Honor Society and the girls' basketball team. She had long wavy auburn hair like their mother's, blue eyes, freckles, and a captivating smile. She was very busy and very popular.

Maggie stopped the car, rolled down the window, and asked, "Brigit, some of my friends and I are going to Meg's Point Beach this afternoon to fly kites. Pete asked me if you would like to come with us."

Brigit was in shock. She was three years younger than Maggie and her friends. Brigit thought Peter Murphy was the most talented junior at Farmington High School. He was the star of all the school plays and wrote amazing poetry for the high school literary magazine. "Now," she thought, "with his imagination, he could grow strawberries."

Brigit was scared to death at the thought of going to the beach with Peter Murphy, Maggie, and her friends. She was sure her mother would never let her go. Actually, that was a comforting thought.

"Brigit!" Maggie called, "I have to go to work. Tell me. Do you want to go kite flying at the beach with us this afternoon?"

Brigit, now called to attention, said, "Mom will never let me go."

"I asked Mom and Dad at breakfast this morning when you went for your walk outside. Daddy said he likes Pete. He has seen him in class plays and sporting

Patricia Clark Smith.

events. He said Pete has always been a gentleman when he stops by the house with my friends. He also admires his acting and poetry. Mom agreed and said as long as you would be with me it would be all right. Brigit, I have to go!" Maggie said impatiently.

For a minute Brigit couldn't breath. She had to make a snap decision. "Yes, yes, I'll go," she said without further thought. As soon as Maggie heard that she started to back out of the driveway. Brigit ran beside the car for a minute or so, "What time? What do I wear? I don't have a kite!" she hollered.

"Don't worry about it. I'll be home at noon. They're picking us up around 12:30 p.m., and they have the kites," Maggie hollered back as she drove down the street.

Brigit stood on the side of the road: numb, bewildered, and a little scared. She, Brigit Clark, was going to the beach with Maggie, her friends, and Peter Murphy. She walked back to the house and into the kitchen.

"A morning walk seems to agree with you, Brigit," her mother said. "How are the strawberry plants doing?"

As Brigit waltzed around the kitchen she wondered out loud, "Why don't you plant strawberries from seeds? Why do you have to start with the plant? Where did strawberries originally come from? And," she said with a twinkle in her eyes, "What should I wear to go kite flying at the beach?" Brigit screamed with delight and jumped up and down while hugging her mother. "Thank you for letting me go to the beach on a date with Maggie and her friends." Then, she collapsed in a kitchen chair with a big smile on her face.

"Brigit, it's not really a date. From what Maggie told us, a bunch of her friends are going kite flying. They invited you to join them. Your father and I agreed partly because Maggie would be with you, and we know how much you love the beach. We know you have missed being near the water this winter. This is a chance for you to be by the water. Peter Murphy is a nice young man. He has always been a gentleman. We believe you are mature for your age, and we trust you know how to behave," Brigit's mother said in a very serious tone. "Wear casual, warm clothes. The beach is a windy and cold place in March," she added. Then she smiled and hugged Brigit, "And, have a lot of fun."

*****

Brigit hopped up the stairs to her bedroom happy and full of high expectations for her afternoon at Meg's Point. Taking off her sweatshirt, she noticed the pink Twomanno pearl hanging from a gold chain around her neck. She sat on her bed and held it gently in her hand.

Brigit's thoughts drifted to Baiting Hollow, to Kevin O'Connell, and the secret her younger sister, Barbara, and she knew about the Twomey legacy. Remembering that Kevin had told her she was the adopted daughter of Abigail Twomanno,

the mermaid, and descendent of Queen
Twomanno, Queen of all the merpeople,
set her mind reeling with memories of her
family's two week vacation to Baiting Hollow
last summer. She remembered the night
by the bonfire when Kevin explained how
Baiting Hollow was the secret passageway
for merbabies wearing the pink Twomanno
pearl to become human and live with
adoptive parents among the Baiting Hollow
beach people. She was proud to know her
mother was one of the Twomey daughters,
descendent of Queen Twomanno, who
greeted Abigail, accepted merbabies, and
promised to provide love and sanctuary for

them. She remembered the promise she made to Kevin to only tell one person the secret of the Baiting Hollow merpeople. Brigit was glad she had shared her secret with her younger sister, Barbara. Barbara was the best at keeping secrets.

Brigit lie across her bed, closed her eyes, and was once again walking to the creek, swimming at sunset, and sitting around a bonfire at night in Baiting Hollow with Barbara, her cousins, and friends. She could feel the warm sand on her feet and the icy cold water surrounding her while swimming. She could hear the seagulls and see orange, pink, and purple colors wash across the sky at sunset on Long Island Sound. In three months Brigit's family would head back to Long Island for their two week vacation with the Twomey relatives and friends in Baiting Hollow and the Twomey farmhouse in Calverton. She waited all winter to return to Long Island for her summer vacation.

All of a sudden Brigit sat up straight, "Oh, my goodness. What if someone throws me in the water while we're at Meg's Point?" Brigit knew that the power of the pink Twomanno pearl would turn her into her mermaid form if she was wearing it while swimming in salt water. "Oh, my goodness!

Oh, my goodness! What will I do?" She took a deep breath and for the first time since last July, Brigit took the necklace with the pink Twomanno pearl off. She held it in her hand, stared at it, and cried. She thought she would wear it forever. Now, faced with the possibility of others' discovering the secret, she worried about wearing it to the beach. She almost did not want to go.

Brigit decided then and there to put her necklace back around her neck. Nothing could make her deny her legacy, not a day at Meg's Point and, no, not even Peter Murphy.

As Brigit continued to get washed and dressed her mind drifted again to Baiting Hollow and her longing to return to the beach and the Twomey farmhouse.

*****

Brigit did not say a word on the ride to the beach and all day flying kites. She thought and thought of something to say, but all she could do was smile when Pete looked at her or spoke to her. Brigit wanted to be in Baiting Hollow.

It was a magnificent day at the beach. The sun was shining. The wind blew hard and steady off the sound. The waves were high and pounded the beach. Pete was by her side. He showed her how to assemble their kite. She sat and watched him demonstrate how to fly it. Then he called her over to him to take a turn. He told her exactly what to do. Then, to her surprise, he stood behind her with his arms holding her arms to help her maneuver the kite. "Oh my," she thought.

After several hours of kite flying, other couples started to wander down the beach. Pete suggested Brigit and he sit on the blanket he brought.

As they sat down, Pete took a pad of
paper and a pencil from his backpack.
He stared at Brigit with a smile. Brigit lay
on her stomach and faced the sound. Her
thoughts and heart drifted again to Baiting
Hollow. She imagined the blanket they were
on was a magic carpet carrying them across
the sound to Baiting Hollow. She wanted
Pete to know all about her wonderful friends
and the Twomey relatives, but Brigit did not
speak.

After a few minutes she turned to look at
Pete. He was writing. He looked at her and
smiled. She smiled back then turned and
looked out across the water again. The

sun was setting. Brigit couldn't wait to see if the sunset on Long Island Sound looked different from the Connecticut shore. Little puffs of pink and orange clouds started to fill the western sky.

Without a word, Pete handed Brigit a folded piece of paper. They both smiled. Brigit opened the paper and read the poem he had written to her.

The Girl on the Sand
The wind, the sea, the sun are there,
And so is she at whom I stare.
Her hair misty brown and blowing free.
Her eyes as blue and deep as the sea,
So quiet and shy wherever she goes,
What she is thinking, no one knows.

Brigit finished reading and closed her eyes. She thought to herself, "Mom was wrong. I am too young. I don't know what to say, what to do, where to look. I wish she never let me come here today." For the first time Brigit spoke, "Thank you, Pete. Your poem is beautiful."

Pete smiled, "I'm glad you like it."

The ride home from the beach was quiet. Brigit sat next to Pete in the back set of Jason's car. Maggie sat in the front seat next to her boy friend, Jason.

When they got to the house, Pete stepped out of the car, held the door for Brigit, and walked her to the front door. Brigit thanked Pete for a wonderful day at the beach. He leaned closer, kissed her on her cheek, and they both said good night.

Brigit's mother greeted her at the front door and asked, "Did you have a nice time?" Brigit nodded, but before she could comment her mother added, "We have company. Come into the living room, say hello to your Uncle David, and give him a kiss."

Brigit smiled and walked into the living room where her father and Uncle David were sitting. Uncle David stood up as Brigit came into the room. She threw her arms around him and gave him a kiss. He gave her a big hug and a kiss, too. Then she went to her father seated in his easy chair, gave him a kiss, and sat next to him on the arm of his chair.

"Uncle David, it is so good to see you. I didn't know you were coming for a visit," Brigit said.

Uncle David explained that he was going to an antique car show in Massachusetts with his Model A Ford and thought he would stop by and say hello on his way. He asked, "Will we see you at the farm when

Patricia Clark Smith.

school gets out? The first two weeks of June are strawberry picking time. Aunt Mame and I would love to have you, Maggie, and Barbara come for a visit. Mame would love your help with the picking, preserving, and freezing of the strawberries the way your mother use to help. There is so much to do when the strawberries are ready for harvest. Aunt Mame always said that having her nieces working with her on the jam made it much sweeter."

"Oh Mom, may we? May we go to the farm for the first two weeks of June for the strawberry harvest?" Brigit begged.

Her mother smiled, nodded, and said, "Well, since it has been a mild winter with no snow days off from school, the last day of school is early June. If it is all right with your father, I think you could go for the second week of the harvest."

Brigit looked at her father with big cow eyes, tilted her head a little to be cute, smiled, and said, "Please, Daddy."

He smiled at her and said, "Of course. I know you love the beach and the farm, and it is important for you to be there as much as possible." Brigit wasn't sure exactly what her father meant by that but was thrilled he agreed to let her go.

Brigit knew there was no arguing with her mother about getting out of school early for the strawberry harvest. Just being at the Twomey farm for the second half of the strawberry harvest was a dream come true.

Her mother added, "I know Maggie will be working full time when school gets out, so she will not be able to go for a week. I am sure Barbara would like to go with you. David, if I drop the girls off at the Cross Island Ferry in New London the second

Friday in June, would you be able to pick them up at Orient Point?"

"Absolutely, you just call, make the arrangements, and let me know the date and time they will arrive and the date and time they will need to return," Uncle David said.

Uncle David then looked at Brigit very seriously and said, "You will have to work very hard. The strawberry harvest is back breaking work, but the rewards are sweet and delicious and make it all worthwhile. Mame always takes a ride up to Aunt Agatha's bungalow in Baiting Hollow after a day of strawberry picking. She usually leaves me a cold sandwich plate, salad, and strawberry shortcake with real cream for my dinner. Agatha has dinner ready for her. They enjoy a swim together and then dinner. Mame's and Agatha's favorite time of the day is early evening, watching the sunset on the horizon of the sound. Agatha always said it was God's everyday masterpiece, a blessing on the day. I know Brigit and Barbara will want to know there is time built in for a swim, dinner with their aunts, and some fun at the beach with their cousins and friends." Uncle David smiled and winked at Brigit.

A flash went through Brigit, realizing for the first time that Uncle David might know the secret of Baiting Hollow. "Oh my," she thought. Then she asked, "Uncle David, why don't you ever go to the beach for a swim?"

"Oh," Uncle David tossed his head from side to side, rubbed his chin, then nodded saying, "I don't really like the beach in summer: the sun, all the people, sand gets into everything. I like to go to the beach in the late fall, winter, and early spring. My job in the family has always been to guard the beach from sharks. Yes, that's my job. Every winter several of the year-round Baiting Hollow beach people like Kevin,

Bobby, and Brendan call me because of shark sightings. Sharks usually come into the sound during the late fall and winter when the ocean starts getting wild and cold."

"During the spring and summer my red pick-up truck is equipped with farm tools. During the fall and winter I keep a small outboard motorboat, my diving suit, deep sea diving equipment, and a stun gun in my truck. When I get a call, I am all set. I drive up to Baiting Hollow, and Kevin, Brendan, Bobby, Peter, Roger, Paul, and sometimes a few other men are ready to help me lift the boat out of the truck and into the water.

I suit up and head out to the Race. I use sonar equipment to locate the sharks. When they are located, I drop anchor and dive into the school of sharks with my stun gun. After a few jolts from my gun, they swim away and back to the open ocean. There are fewer and fewer shark sightings every winter. Over the years they have learned to stay out of the sound."

"Oh, my goodness! Uncle David, you are so brave," Brigit exclaimed.

Uncle David answered, "On the farm everybody has jobs to do. The Baiting Hollow beach people have depended on the Twomey family to keep the sharks out of Long Island Sound for over a hundred years, since my grandparents first settled in Baiting Hollow in 1860 from Ireland. Pop and all my brothers have helped out from time to time. Pop told me that kindness is essential to a strawberry farmer's success. Since I am the last Twomey brother at the farm, the job is mine. The Twomeys have always had a special relationship with the Baiting Hollow beach people. They are like family to us."

Then Brigit asked, "Has there ever been a shark attack in Baiting Hollow?"

There was a long pause. Brigit saw her Uncle look at her Mother. She saw her mother shake her head from side to side and another long pause. Uncle David stared at Lillian, Brigit's mother. She finally took a deep breath and said, "OK, if you must tell her. I guess she has a right to know."

"What?" Brigit asked.

"Brigit, do you remember the terrible storm this past December on the day after Christmas?" Uncle David asked seriously.

"You mean the nor'easter that hit New England and Long Island?" she responded.

"Yes. Well, let's see. Where do I begin? The night of the storm I was sitting in my reclining chair in the living room at home watching the news and the weather report: eighteen to twenty inches of snow and gale force winds. I knew it was bad outside. The wind was howling, and the snow was coming down in huge flakes against the window. All of a sudden, within the howling of the wind, I heard the banshee wail. I felt my blood turn to ice water."

"What's a banshee?" Brigit interrupted.

"Brigit, I thought you knew about the Twomey banshee," her father inquired.

"No, I have never heard of it. What is it?" she demanded.

Her father explained, "In Ireland, all the families had a banshee assigned to them to warn family members if a relative was in danger of dying. It is an ancient Irish fairy. She appears as an old woman ghost with long scraggly gray hair, a silver hair comb given to her from Zeus, and a flowing gray hooded gown. The banshee sits on tree tops and hilltops near her assigned family."

Uncle David interrupted and continued, "When your great grandparents, John and Elizabeth Doherty Twomey, came from

Patricia Clark Smith.

Ireland in 1860 and settled in Baiting Hollow, the Twomey banshee came with them and settled in Baiting Hollow, too. When they bought the Twomey homestead and farm on Twomey Avenue in the latter 1860's, the Twomey banshee moved closer to the farmhouse. That old ghost now watches over relatives from Baiting Hollow, Calverton, Riverhead, and all across Suffolk County, Long Island."

Brigit interrupted, "Where does the Twomey banshee live?"

"Oh, let's see," Uncle David thought for a minute.

"Brigit," her mother called her attention to her. "She has been seen in the Baiting Hollow cliffs sitting on the roof tops of cottages. She has also been seen in the treetops by Banshee Curve just north of the Twomey farm. You drive north on Twomey Avenue from the farm and take a right on Young Road. Young Road winds and curves up then to the right then to the left and down a tall hill. It marks the northern boundary of the Twomey farm. She is usually there. If you look up in the trees on a night that the stars are out and the moon is bright you can see her."

"Oh my, that is where Aunt Mame, Barbara, and I go to pick strawberries," Brigit stated in astonishment that she knew and had been exactly where the banshee resided but never knew that this old spirit was there.

Lillian continued, "When I was a teenager I remember visiting Uncle Dan Kaelin and his family on Roanoke Avenue which runs parallel to Twomey Avenue. We had a nice dinner, and then I played cards with my cousin, Mary. I always had a lot of fun with Mary. My Uncle Dan loved to tell stories. Around 10:00 p.m., I said I had better get home, that Mom was expecting me. Uncle Dan asked how I planned to drive home. I said by way of the short cut on Young Road. It was then that Uncle Dan told me to drive carefully around Banshee Curve. He raised his eye brows and told me that the old banshee will be sitting up in the tree tops. Uncle Dan said that if I look up at her, she will come swooping down on me wailing her blood curdling wails. I told him I would drive carefully and keep my eyes on the road. Well, I did, and I made it home safely but trembling with fear all the way."

"Why does a family need a banshee?" Brigit asked.

Uncle David continued the story, "The banshee warns families of the imminent death of a family member by her wailing. If the family can rescue the dying person, the death coach will not come. According to legend once the death coach is sent out, it will not return without a soul. One night when I was a little boy, our mother was awakened from a deep sleep by the wailing of the Twomey banshee. Mom quickly went from room to room to check on each of her children. When she went back to bed, she said her prayers. In the morning she heard from a neighbor that sadly a second cousin on the Twomey side of the family living in

Riverhead had almost lost a baby in child birth the night before." Brigit's eyes were as big as saucers. Her mouth hung open in disbelief. "Brigit would you rather I did not go on?" Uncle David asked.

"No, please, tell me what happened with you and the banshee this winter," Brigit insisted.

"Well, as I was saying, just as I heard the banshee wailing, the phone rang. It was Kevin O'Connell calling from Baiting Hollow. He begged me to come down to Baiting Hollow immediately. He was awakened by the banshee's wailing. His parents were still sleeping. Through the porch window he could see the storm swirling and hear the wind gusts blowing and rattling the shutters on the cottage. He opened the front door of his family's home and strained to look out through the whiteout conditions caused by the storm. In the swirling snow storm, over the pounding of the surf, he heard an unnatural thrashing just off shore. He said he thought he heard a woman crying for help and knew he had to call me. I assured him I would be there as soon as I could and asked him to phone Bobby before I arrived. You see, Brigit, it was important for us to save this person in danger before the death coach arrived to take her soul away from this world."

Uncle David continued, "Kevin said they would meet me at the boat launch, so I didn't waste any time. I grabbed my coat and flew out the door to my truck. By the time I arrived in Baiting Hollow, Bobby and Kevin were just arriving at the boat launch area. We stared at the wild storm on the sound. I had to yell over the storm to them to help me carry the boat to the water. Without saying a word Bobby pointed to a lifeless form he noticed lying on the large exposed boulder of the jetty in front of the O'Connell's bungalow about ten feet from the high tide waters on shore. The beach and jetty were being pounded with high waves."

Uncle David paused and took a deep breath. He rearranged himself on his chair and went on, "I jumped out of the truck. We tried to make out in the darkness what was draped across the jetty. Right in front of our eyes a large, powerful dolphin leaped out of the water and landed next to the form. The dolphin seemed to gently nuzzle the body. We wondered if it was another dolphin that had been attacked by sharks."

Then Uncle David told Brigit, Lillian, and Al what he witnessed, "Within a few seconds, we saw the silhouetted form of a woman pull herself onto the back of the great gray dolphin. The wind howled, the waves pounded the shore and the jetty, the snow poured out of the heavens, and the dolphin with what looked like a mermaid on his back slipped off the jetty and disappeared into the wild, dark, and mysterious Long Island Sound."

Everyone sat quietly for a few minutes. No one said a word. Brigit felt her heart pounding under her pink Twomanno pearl. She knew it had to be Abigail and Daniel

45

who Bobby, Kevin, and Uncle David had seen on the jetty during that terrible storm. She couldn't wait to return to Long Island, to the farm, and to Baiting Hollow. She had to find out what happened. Brigit wondered if Abigail was trying to get a message to the Baiting Hollow beach people. "Something is wrong," she thought, "Abigail needs my help."

Brigit heard Uncle David continue his story, "Bobby, Kevin, and I looked at each other. Bobby and Kevin wanted to go out in my boat to check for sharks. I had never heard of a shark attack so close to the beach. I tried to convince them not to go out

46

in the storm that night. Kevin said those sharks could not think that they could get away with an attack in Baiting Hollow. Kevin told Bobby to warn the other Baiting Hollow beach people of the shark attack and told me to go back to the farmhouse. He said he'd call us when he returned. To this day we haven't heard from Kevin, and no one has seen him since that night." Uncle David put his head in his hands and started to cry, "I knew I shouldn't have let him go without me."

*****

The spring passed slowly with sadly no news from Uncle David about Kevin. Lillian, Al, Maggie, Brigit, and Barbara prayed for Kevin's safe return to Baiting Hollow. Finally, summer vacation had arrived. It was the second week of June, time for the strawberry harvest.

Brigit's mother drove Brigit and Barbara to the 3:30 p.m. New London Cross Island Ferry. They were looking forward to their week on the Twomey farm and were determined to find out about Kevin O'Connell.

Brigit and Barbara stood at the front
of the ferry boat as it crossed Long Island
Sound. Their hands firmly grasped hold of
the piped railing, their feet squarely planted
on the deck, and their eyes focused on the
sliver of Long Island they could see on the
horizon. It was a wild and windy ride across
the sound as they approached Orient Point.
"Hold on tightly, Barbara," Brigit directed
her younger sister. "Are you all right? Do
you want to go inside?"

"Are you kidding? This is so exciting!
What a ride!" Barbara screamed with
excitement! Then she softly added, "I've
been scanning the water looking for some

Patricia Clark Smith.

sign of Kevin or maybe Abigail. I know Daniel would never let anything happen to them." Brigit put her arm around her sister, and together they watched the water.

Brigit looked ahead and saw the ferry pass the black and white Orient Point lighthouse and approach the docking station. Barbara took one more look out at the sound hoping Kevin had found his way back to Baiting Hollow. She knew he was a merperson of Baiting Hollow, and he would be safe.

The sun was shining, the sky was blue, and the air was as clean and fresh as could be. Brigit closed her eyes and inhaled deeply. She was so happy to be back on Long Island. There was work to do, work her mother and relatives had done for generations: strawberries to pick; jam to preserve; shortcake to cook; and a mermaid, dolphin, and dear friend to save.

When the ferry bumped into the dock, Brigit and Barbara spied Uncle David. They waved and jumped up and down until he saw them and waved back. The drawbridge of the ferry lowered, and Brigit and Barbara ran off the ferry with their suitcases in tow to their uncle's arms. He gave them both a big hug and kiss. "How was your trip across the sound?" he asked. The two girls told him all about their ride. "Mame and I are so happy you could come for the week. Mame has your bedroom all ready. She went shopping this morning for groceries, jars, paraffin, and other ingredients needed for making strawberry jam and shortcake."

Barbara and Brigit jumped into Uncle David's Model A rumble seat Ford: Brigit in the front seat and Barbara in the rumble seat. Uncle David drove west, Route 25 turned into Sound Avenue. Brigit and Barbara quietly took in all the familiar sights and sounds of eastern Long Island. It was a beautiful day, breezy and sunny.

Barbara commented, "The light is different here on the Island. Everything is clean, clear, and fresh. Mmm, it is so good to be back on Long Island, back home."

Uncle David's car drove past acres of potato fields. Brigit recognized the early potato and corn plants. Farmers driving their tractors waved as Uncle David drove by, and he honked the car horn to them in return. Everyone seemed to know Uncle David.

"There's your Aunt Alice's and Uncle Lyndon's house on the right. If you look out in the field, I think that's your cousin,

Henry, on the tractor," Uncle David said as he pointed proudly to his nephew out in the field. Uncle David honked the horn, and Henry waved and smiled from his tractor continuing along the rows of potato plants. Brigit and Barbara hung out of the car, smiled, waved, and hollered, "Hi, Henry! We love you!"

Along the road a large mimosa tree dripping with fluffy pink blossoms alerted Brigit that Uncle David would be turning south on Twomey Avenue. She couldn't wait to see the family farm, barn, and house. Driving down Twomey Avenue, Brigit noticed the turn for Young Road and remembered the banshee story Uncle David, her mother, and her father had told her last March. She smiled as the car continued past the irrigation system. Brigit loved listening to the rhythmic swish, swish of the irrigation system's watering the new crop of potatoes.

"I spy the barn!" Barbara yelled. Startled, Brigit looked south and saw the, oh so familiar, gigantic tan Twomey barn with its signature green roof just ahead. Her heart leaped for joy. Uncle David turned in the driveway by the barn and drove past the chicken coop, tool shed, and garage.

As he approached the back of the family home, Brigit saw Mame in her flower garden on the side of the house. Mame stood up and waved her apron as she always did to welcome family and friends. As soon as the car stopped, Brigit and Barbara ran to Aunt Mame and gave her hugs and kisses. Putting her arms around her nieces, Mame held a bouquet of daisies in one hand and her garden scissors in the other.

"Oh, it's so good to see you," Mame said. "How was your ride across the sound on the ferry?"

"It was wonderful: sunny, windy, lots of white caps and puffy clouds," Barbara answered. "We even saw a school of dolphins leaping in and out of the water in the Race."

"Well, let's go inside, get you settled, and I want to hear all about your Mom, Dad, and Maggie. It's so nice to have you home for a visit," Mame said.

As the girls brought their suitcases upstairs, the phone rang. Mame hurried to the phone at the foot of the staircase, picked up the receiver, and said, "Hello." After a short pause, the girls heard Mame say, "Oh, that's great, Barbara and Brigit Clark are visiting for the week. I know they will be happy to know you are out at the bungalow. We'll come up to the beach for a visit later. I'll let David know the boys will help move irrigation pipes with him tomorrow." Aunt Mame hung up and called upstairs, "Brigit, Barbara, that was Aunt Agatha. The Meyers are in Baiting Hollow. They are opening the bungalow for the summer and asked if we'd like to come for a visit and a swim later."

Before she finished, both girls yelled back, "Yes! Yes! Oh, what fun it will be to see everyone." They dropped their bags on the floor and did a little mermaid dance

of joy around the room over the kitchen.

Barbara started to sing to the tune of "The

Farmer in the Dell":

> We're going to the beach,
> We're going to the beach,
> High, ho, the dario,
> We're going to the beach.

Then Brigit followed singing:

> The merqueen picks the dolphin,
> The merqueen picks the dolphin,
> High, ho, the dario,
> The merqueen picks the dolphin.

They looped arms and Barbara continued:

> The dolphin picks the mermaid,
> The dolphin picks the mermaid,
> High, ho, the dario,
> The dolphin picks the mermaid.

Barbara and Brigit then separated from
each other, leaped, twirled, and sang:

> The mermaid picks the merlord,
> The mermaid picks the merlord,
> High, ho, the dario,
> The mermaid picks the merlord.

They paused, dancing now in place, while
clapping their hands over their heads, and
singing:

> The merlord stands alone,
> The merlord stands alone,
> High, ho, the dario,
> The merlord stands alone.

They clapped frantically, laughing and
giggling at their silly dance of joy and
collapsed on the floor. Someone's clapping

at the door surprised them. They turned to see Aunt Mame, "Well, if there were any Twomey ghosts, you certainly scared them away."

"Ghosts?" Barbara and Brigit gasped.

"No, no. Now, don't start thinking like that. I was just teasing. It is so good to have you here filling the old house with joy. You reminded me of the fun I used to have with your Mom and all my sisters and brothers when we were young. Why don't you finish unpacking, get washed up, and I'll get dinner on the table?" Mame suggested.

"We'll be down in a minute to help," Barbara said as she stood up and went to hug Aunt Mame one more time. Brigit gave Aunt Mame a hug, too, "It is so good to be home."

When Barbara and Brigit came downstairs they couldn't believe their eyes. Mame had the dining room table set with Grandma Twomey's best china with fancy gold trim. She had a beautiful pink linen table cloth, matching linen napkins, a huge bouquet of daisies in a vase in the center of the table with two pink tapered candles on either side of the flower arrangement. At the head of the table sat Uncle David, himself, ready to eat.

Mame came into the dining room with a huge platter of roast beef, potatoes, and carrots piping hot from the kitchen. "Welcome girls. We are so happy to have you here with us," she said as she placed the platter of food on the table. The two sisters were so happy, "Thank you for having us," they answered.

"OK, OK, let's eat," Uncle David directed as he started to bless himself and say grace, "Bless us, Oh Lord, and these they gifts, which we are about to receive, from thy bounty, through Christ our Lord, Amen."

"Amen!" Mame, Barbara, and Brigit echoed. It was a wonderful dinner: roast beef from the butcher, potatoes and carrots from the farm, fresh milk from their cow, homemade biscuits with real butter, and Aunt Mame's homemade banana cream pie for dessert. Brigit and Barbara told Uncle David and Aunt Mame all about the Clarks' news from Connecticut, the strawberry patch in their back yard, and the school year. They heard news about all the Long Island relatives and how well the Twomey strawberry crop was doing this year. They discussed the plans to get up early tomorrow morning and go strawberry picking, come home, make jam, and then go to the beach for a picnic dinner. Uncle David was pleased to learn from Aunt Mame that Albert, David, and Brendan were going to help him move irrigation pipes tomorrow.

The table was cleared by the girls while Uncle David retired to the living room, and Aunt Mame started to put the food away from dinner. After the kitchen was cleaned, they were going to the beach.

*****

It was almost 8:00 p.m. when Aunt Mame, Brigit, and Barbara arrived in Baiting Hollow. Mame parked her car behind the Meyer's bungalow, and the two girls opened their car doors and hopped out. They met Mame at the trunk to get their beach towels and help carry some of Mame's bags into the bungalow. As Mame slammed the trunk closed they looked up to see Aunt Agatha at the back door of the bungalow waving and smiling. The girls followed Mame across the slate steps through the sand to the steps and on the back deck.

"Welcome, welcome! It's so good to see you," Aunt Agatha said as she gave Mame, Barbara, and Brigit hugs and kisses. "Come on in. You girls probably want to put on your bathing suits and go for a swim before it gets too dark. We all worked hard today opening and cleaning out the bungalow and raking the sand outside clean of seaweed and debris from the winter. Uncle Joe, Uncle Chris, Sonny, Richie, and Bobbie came up to the beach today and helped David and Albert put the raft out in the water. Now, the boys are all gathering driftwood for the bonfire," Aunt Agatha explained.

As Aunt Mame and Aunt Agatha settled on the porch, Brigit and Barbara walked out the front porch screen door. They paused at the top of the steps for a minute to survey the beach and the water. A bright candy apple red sun was descending in the western horizon of Long Island Sound. Orange, yellow, and purple filled the sky and water along the massive cliffs which surrounded Baiting Hollow. Brigit was mesmerized once again by the beauty of the sunset in Baiting Hollow. This little beach which she loved so much was truly a little piece of Heaven on earth.

"Hey Brigit, the beach kids are walking from the creek," Barbara announced and tugged at Brigit's arm as she started down the front stairs of the bungalow. Brigit looked and saw David, Albert, Peter, Paul, Roger, and the other beach kids carrying arms full of wood and dragging long driftwood logs behind them. They waved while crossing the jetty between the O'Connell's and Meyer's bungalows. The girls ran to help them.

Once they were in front of the bungalow, Brigit and Barbara stood back to watch David and Albert build the wooden structure. David suggested that everyone

Patricia Clark Smith.

find some smaller pieces of wood. Albert,
Barbara, and Brigit spread out and
searched the jetties, around and under the
bungalows, and along the high water mark
for wood, and returned to David with the
driftwood. Albert ran into the bungalow and
came out with old newspaper and matches
which he gave to David to start the fire.

The driftwood took the form of an eight
foot teepee filled with kindling and paper.
"Everyone, stand back while I light the fire,"
David ordered. The sun had set below the
horizon, and the beach was dark when
David struck the match and lit the fire.
Within seconds, red and orange flames

licked the rough driftwood, and the bonfire roared. Everyone found a place to sit. Soon other Baiting Hollow beach residents came out of their bungalows to enjoy the bonfire. Aunt Agatha and Aunt Mame brought a bag of marshmallows for everyone to roast on sticks over the bonfire.

The first bonfire marked the beginning of the summer of 1961. Now, the bonfire roared and lit the night with a bright orange and yellow light. The gentle high tide waves rhythmically lapped the beach. Around the fire were generations of Baiting Hollow beach friends and Twomey relatives. This is what Brigit had waited for all winter.

For the moment things seemed almost too perfect, when Brigit noticed an unusual stillness: no laughing or teasing, no storytelling, no one was being thrown in the water. Brigit also noticed the tide had not changed in ten or fifteen minutes. Kevin O'Connell told her last summer that there was a quiet and still time, about twenty minutes long, between the tides called slack tide when the tides stood still. He said it was a time of enchantment. Noticing the slack tide for the first time only made it seem like an omen of something horrible to come. She suddenly realized that Kevin O'Connell was nowhere to be seen. "David, do you know where Kevin is? It's not like him not to attend the first bonfire of the summer," Brigit asked. David turned his attention from the bonfire, looked at Brigit, then looked away toward the sound. "What is the matter, Albert?" Brigit asked. He too cast his eyes aside and looked out over the water without a word. She had never seen her cousins look so serious and sad.

The other beach kids turned, looked at Brigit and then to David and Albert waiting for an answer. Staring out on the water, Bobby started talking, "Sixty mile per hour winds ripped though Baiting Hollow. The giant waves pounded the shore.

Patricia Clark Smith.

Snow poured out of the heavens. And, the banshee wailed a deafening cry. I woke up to a phone call from Kevin telling me to meet Uncle David and him at the boat launch. I ran out the front door. Mother Nature had unleashed her wrath on Baiting Hollow. From my bungalow I thought I heard thrashing in the water and a cry. I headed down the beach to the boat launch. By the time I was there Kevin had arrived, and Uncle David was backing his truck down the boat launch. I hollered to them and pointed through the blinding swirling darkness to show them a lifeless figure I just noticed draped across the second jetty."

Bobby paused, looked down for a moment, and then continued, "Just then what appeared to be a large dolphin leaped to the jetty. The figure reached and pulled herself onto the back of the great dolphin, and then they slipped into the raging waters. Worried that someone had been attacked by a shark, Kevin jumped into Uncle David's boat and demanded that he take it out alone. He would not let Uncle David or me come with him. It was hopeless. The waves slammed the little boat. I ran back to my bungalow, went directly to the living room hutch, and took a small coral chest from the top drawer and opened it. I saw two precious pink pearls on gold chains. I lifted one out of the chest and placed it around my neck."

"I ran out the door and down the road to the beach, across the jetty, and dove into the icy sound. The water was dark and turbulent. In my merman form I was able to stay underwater with the current and search for Kevin."

"About an hour out at sea, I was greeted by the seven dolphin Guardians from Queen Daphnia, Queen of all the Dolphins. They told me that the Queen had sent them to let the Baiting Hollow beach people know that

Abigail and Daniel had been attacked by
sharks in the sound and were healing in her
castle. Queen Daphnia asked that I return
to Baiting Hollow and warn the beach
people to stay out of the water. She told me
to get David Twomey to once again chase
the sharks out of the sound."

"I asked if they had seen or heard any
news about Kevin O'Connell. The seven
Guardians said they haven't heard anything
but would definitely continue looking for
him. They were sure he would follow the
same route which brought Brigit and him
to the castle last summer. Following Queen
Daphnia's orders as the Guardians had

explained I reluctantly returned to Baiting Hollow.

"We all trusted that David Twomey, Long Island Sound's greatest shark hunter, would make the sound free of sharks. Since then every morning at sunrise David came to Baiting Hollow, met me, and we went shark hunting and searched for any sign of Kevin. We combed every inch of the sound from the boat and under the sea. When we came across a shark we hit it with his stun gun. It would yelp and swim away. We haven't seen a shark since the end of April and believe the sound is once again free of sharks."

Bobby paused and said, "It is late now. I know you are all helping Aunt Mame, Uncle David, and Uncle Johnny with the strawberry harvest and the moving of irrigation pipes tomorrow, so we better call it a night." Only a few red embers remained from the bonfire. David got the bucket from under the bungalow and went to the water's edge to fill it with water, while Albert started to push sand around and over the remainder of the fire. Bobby stood and noticed tears in Barbara's eyes. He took her hand to help her up, walked her to the bungalow stairs, and said, "Don't worry. We are going to find Kevin, and everything will be fine. It is going to be a wonderful summer. You'll see. I promise." The first bonfire of summer was over, but the summer of 1961 had just begun.

*****

The next morning, sleeping in the room over the kitchen, Brigit and Barbara awoke to the easy hum of Aunt Mame's and Uncle David's talking. They could smell the aroma of fried eggs, bacon, and fresh perked coffee. As Brigit opened her eyes she could see the sunshine from eastern Long Island pour in the bedroom and hear the chirping of birds and the mooing of the family cows.

It was a perfect summer morning. All of a sudden she remembered that Barbara and she were going to help Aunt Mame with the strawberry harvest, sat up, and called, "Barbara, Barbara, we have to get up."

Barbara sat up and without a word went to the bathroom to start getting ready. Brigit opened the curtains and enjoyed the morning breeze coming in the window. She closed her eyes and said her morning prayers, "Thank you, God, for this beautiful day; for my family, relatives, and friends; and for your blessing on the strawberry harvest today. And, please help Kevin return safely to his family and friends in Baiting Hollow."

The sound of a car coming in the stone driveway interrupted Brigit's prayer. It stopped in back of the house, and David, Albert, and Brendan stepped out, slammed the car doors, and headed up the back stoop through the lobby, and into the kitchen. Brigit heard all the excitement of their arrival. Mame offered the boys coffee and breakfast and promised them a noontime feast of baked chicken, potatoes, carrots, and homemade apple pie. The boys knew that the best part of helping Uncle David move irrigation pipe was enjoying

Aunt Mame's cooking. As soon as Barbara
came out of the bathroom, Brigit went in.
Barbara made the bed and tidied up the
room while waiting for Brigit. She looked
in the mirror above the vanity to comb her
long curly red hair, noticed the statue of
St. Theresa, the Little Flower, and said her
prayer, "St. Theresa, please pick me a rose
from the Heavenly garden and send it to me
with a message of God's love. Please dear
God, return Kevin safely to his family and
friends in Baiting Hollow."

The boys headed out the door with Uncle
David just as the girls came downstairs.
Aunt Mame greeted them, "Good morning,

Glories." The girls gave Mame a big hug and kiss and sat down to the hearty breakfast Mame had prepared for them. Mame sat with her cup of coffee and shared some of the morning news. She told them Uncle Johnny is very strict about children coming into the strawberry fields. "Girls, we have to start at the beginning of each row of plants, walk in the path, and be sure not to step on the berries and plants. You'll squat and bend over the plants. As you lift the tiny leaves, clusters of berries will be revealed. Only pick the ripe red berries, not the over-ripe or damaged berries or the white and orange ones. We'll wear the straw hats that are hanging in the lobby to protect us from the sun."

After breakfast, the girls cleared the table and washed and dried the dishes as Mame swept the kitchen floor and put the food away. She then emptied the washing machine, and Brigit and Barbara followed her out to the clothesline to hang the basket of clean wet clothes on the line. Morning chores seemed effortless on such a perfect day.

By 9:00 a.m., Aunt Mame had a piping hot pot of coffee on the stove for Uncle David and the boy's mid-morning break.

Mame, Barbara, and Brigit grabbed their
hats and containers for strawberries and
walked out to the barn. Aunt Mame pushed
the giant barn door to slide it open and
told the girls to wait on the grass while she
backed the car out of the barn. They hopped
in and were off. When they arrived at the
Twomey strawberry field Uncle Johnny
came walking over to greet them. He
welcomed the girls and told Mame there was
a great crop this morning. Brigit surveyed
the rolling field of little plants in neat and
tidy rows. She looked up to the tall pine
trees at the edge of the field to see if she
could spy the Twomey banshee. That

old lady spirit was nowhere to be seen. Mame called to the girls and pointed out where they would begin picking the berries. Barbara swooned as she approached the field, "Oh, Aunt Mame, the air is filled with strawberry perfume, mmm! Is this what Heaven is like?"

"Come back to earth, Barbara," said Aunt Mame. "There will be time for that later. Now, remember it is a privilege to be allowed into the Twomey strawberry fields. You must step carefully and treat each plant delicately so as not to harm a single plant or berry.

Patricia Clark Smith.

The girls agreed and promised to follow Aunt Mame's lead. After a few minutes of picking, Barbara started to hum a little tune. Then she started singing:

> Welcome to the strawberry fields,
> harvest what you may.
> Tiny plants have yielded fruit for you
> to take away.
> Precious berries, ruby red, are sweet
> and juicy fun;
> Strawberry gifts from the earth,
> kissed by the morning sun.
> We'll take them back to the Twomey
> home for a strawberry jubilee.
> Thank you Lord, for this blessing on
> the Twomey family ..."

When Barbara's singing turned back to humming, Aunt Mame interrupted and asked if we ever heard of Grandma Twomey's strawberry juice. The girls looked up from their picking and shook their heads, no. So, Aunt Mame told the story, "Every year during the strawberry harvest, Mom always made jam, shortcake, and strawberry juice for Pop. She stored the juice in large jars and kept them in the cellar on shelves where it was cool. The children knew it was for Pop, and they were not supposed to touch it. Pop told us that Denny, a young boy ghost living in the basement, would chase children if they went into the cellar. So, we never went downstairs."

Patricia Clark Smith.

"One summer day, when your mother, Lillian, was about seven or eight years old, she noticed Joe, our brother, working by himself in the potato field under the noonday sun. Lillian thought he must be very thirsty. She remembered how her mother used to bring strawberry juice from the cool cellar to Pop working in the field. For a minute she remembered the story of Denny, but her love of her brother made her go and get the juice anyway. She grabbed a jar off the shelf, ran upstairs and out of the house into the field where Joe was working. She handed the jar of cool ruby red juice to Joe. He opened it and took a long refreshing gulp. He offered Lillian a drink. She too enjoyed a gulp of Mom's juice. It was heavenly on a summer afternoon. When they finished the jar of juice, Joe thanked Lillian and said he had to get back to work. As Lillian stood up she felt a little dizzy but figured it was from the heat." She went back to the house and up to her room for a little afternoon nap."

"When Lillian woke up she didn't feel very well. She went downstairs to where our mother was working in the kitchen and told her how she was feeling and how she brought Joe a cold drink of strawberry juice the way she had seen Mom bring the same drink to our father on a hot summer afternoon. Mom just smiled and said she would feel better tomorrow."

"Your mother did not know that the juice had fermented and become strawberry wine. She never touched it again. We all laughed and laughed when Lillian told the story at dinner that night".

Mame paused and then asked the girls, "Did you know the strawberry plant is a member of the rose family?" Barbara could not believe it. She told Mame about her morning prayer to St. Theresa, "Please pick me a rose from the Heavenly garden and send it to me as a message of God's love."

"Well, my dear niece, you received a field of little white flowers, roses. You are loved, and your prayer was answered," Aunt Mame exclaimed. Barbara was so happy she thought she was going to cry. She quietly thanked St. Theresa for her field of strawberry roses and could not wait to tell Mom and Dad back in Connecticut.

Back at the farmhouse, Mame and the girls brought their quarts and baskets of strawberries into the lobby and took off their muddy sneakers. The girls and Mame went upstairs to wash. By the time Barbara and Brigit returned to the kitchen, Aunt Mame had started the noon dinner for Uncle David and the boys. She told the girls that after dinner they would make the jam and shortcake. Brigit and Barbara set the kitchen table for seven.

After dinner the boys thanked Mame and headed back to the beach. Uncle David went out to the barn. Barbara and Brigit cleaned up the dishes while Aunt Mame had her coffee and put away the food. The time had come for making the jam. Aunt Mame spread newspaper on the kitchen floor. The girls brought in the containers of strawberries from the lobby and put them on the newspaper as Mame took some large bowls and pots from the pantry. She showed them how to hull and cut each berry and put them in the bowls. When the bowl was full of berries, Mame took it to the sink to wash the berries and then poured them into the huge pot on the stove. She added sugar and pectin. The girls continued to hull and cut the strawberries, while Aunt Mame stirred the boiling mixture. The kitchen was filled with the aroma of sweet strawberries. "Oh, Aunt Mame, it smells so good," Brigit said as she inhaled the fragrance of cooking strawberries. The girls walked over to the stove to watch Mame stir and then scrape the pink foam off the top of the boiling jam mixture. When Mame knew the jam was ready she carefully ladled it into sterile jars and spooned melted paraffin on top of the jam in each jar. Later when they cooled she wiped the sides of the jars and put on the lids.

After making several batches of jam, Aunt Mame made shortcake while the girls continued to hull and cut more berries. "We'll have strawberry shortcake for Uncle David's dinner. He loves it in a bowl with real cream from the top of the cow's milk poured over it. After we clean up we'll go

up to Baiting Hollow to visit Aunt Agatha.
We'll bring her some shortcake, berries,
and cream too. You've both worked so hard
today. Do you think you'd like to go for a
swim later?" Aunt Mame asked.

"Oh, Yes!" both girls yelled out loud.

*****

Aunt Mame pulled her car into her
regular parking place behind the Meyer's
bungalow. The girls jumped out and
slammed the doors to the car behind
them. Aunt Agatha came out the back door
and waved, "I've been waiting all day for
homemade strawberry shortcake. Welcome!"

Barbara and Brigit helped Mame get the berries, shortcake, cream, and beach bags out of the trunk of her car and followed her up to Aunt Agatha by the back door of the bungalow. Aunt Agatha gave everyone kisses and said that the boys were out on the front porch waiting for the strawberry shortcake. Brigit and Barbara walked to the front porch while Aunt Mame and Aunt Agatha prepared the shortcake for the beach kids and themselves in the kitchen. Brigit stepped onto the screen porch and her eyes were drawn to Long Island Sound and the beach. The late afternoon sun created soft silver tips on the dark blue choppy water. Oh, how she longed to run outside and dive into the now high tide water. She looked around the porch to see everyone and said, "Hello." She was ready to burst into the story of the strawberry harvest but stopped short when she saw the very serious faces looking back at her. "What is the matter with everyone?" Barbara blurted out.

Albert spoke, "When we came back to the bungalow after moving irrigation pipes with Uncle David we decided to go for a swim out to the raft. I changed into my trunks and was the first on the beach. Standing at the water's edge I looked up and down the beach and then dove in. I swam to the raft, climbed up, and rested."

"Lying on the raft with my eyes closed enjoying the soft rocking of the waves I was startled by a splash of water. I sat up quickly expecting to see David or Brendan. Was I surprised to see a mermaid! It was Abigail. I was mesmerized by her beauty: long curly red hair; sea blue eyes; and shimmering green, blue, and silver scales. She wore a large pink Twomanno pearl on sea grass around her neck. She told me that she knew all of the beach kids must be worried about Kevin. She said that last winter during a terrible storm, Daniel, the head dolphin, and she were patrolling the waters of Long Island Sound for Lord Lahranno and his band of sharks. This angry merlord has vowed to lure all the land merchildren back to sea and hold them captive until they agree to be loyal to him alone."

"Abigail reported to me that as Daniel and she approached Baiting Hollow, twelve of Lord Lahranno's fiercest sharks suddenly attacked her and threw her up on the second jetty. Daniel and she were caught off guard by the sudden attack. It all happened in a matter of seconds. Daniel started to attack the sharks but stopped to

Patricia Clark Smith.

turn around and rescue Abigail. The sharks
swam out a ways, lurking just beyond the
sand bar. After she climbed onto Daniel's
back, he swam swiftly back to Queen
Daphnia's castle."

Albert continued, "Abigail also said
that the sharks were aware that Uncle
David, Bobby, and Kevin were on the shore
planning to head out in his boat to go after
them the way he always does. They just
watched and waited, biding their time. They
were ordered by Lord Lahranno to capture
the beach kids, and they were determined to
do just that."

Albert said, "Abigail told me that when the sharks saw Kevin head out in Uncle David's boat, they followed him to the open ocean. The twelve sharks then rammed into the boat. Kevin was knocked over, flying out of the boat. Fortunately, he was wearing his pink Twomanno pearl and immediately turned into his merman form as he touched the ocean water. Unfortunately, he hit his head on the boat and was knocked unconscious. The sharks found a rope from the boat floating nearby, tied it around Kevin, and dragged him back to Lord Lahranno's hideaway. Then she told me that Kevin was in a coma for several months and now has amnesia."

"I slid off the raft and swam to Abigail. I put my arms around her. After holding her for a few minutes I asked her how the beach kids could help rescue Kevin. She said that Seamus, the old gardener from Queen Daphnia's castle is operating as a spy for her. He is pretending to be a loyal follower of Lord Lahranno but is keeping Queen Daphnia informed of everything that is going on. Kevin is not in any physical harm while he has amnesia. Lord Lahranno does not want him harmed. He is hoping Kevin will stay with him when he regains his memory."

Albert also said, "Abigail asked me to
tell the beach kids to keep them in their
prayers. She said she knows that Brigit is
especially worried about her merbrother.
She said to tell everyone that Queen
Daphnia, Daniel, the Guardians, all the sea
creatures, and she will never let anything
happen to Kevin. Abigail asked us to please
be patient and pray. She gave me a tight
hug and a kiss and dove back into the
sound."

"I swam back to the raft and climbed
up. I took a deep breath and tried to see if
I could catch one last glimpse of Abigail.
Distracted by David's and Brendan's calls

from shore, I turned to see them dive in and swim to the raft to join me. I didn't know how I was going to tell them what I had just learned from Abigail."

"Coma, amnesia! Albert, what are we going to do?" Brigit demanded.

Albert closed his eyes for a few minutes and then said, "Brigit, Abigail has asked us to pray. That is what we are going to do. I know you believe in the power of prayer. God will take care of Kevin, and he will come back to us." The beach kids sitting on the front porch of the Meyer's bungalow bowed their heads in prayer. Aunt Agatha and Aunt Mame joined them.

Albert was the first one to speak, "Dear God, please keep Kevin safe and bring him back to his family and friends in Baiting Hollow. Amen."

"Amen," was echoed by everyone on the porch.

After a few quiet minutes, Aunt Mame asked, "Who would like some homemade strawberry shortcake with farm fresh cream?"

Everyone perked up and in unison called out, "Me!"

Aunt Agatha helped Aunt Mame bring bowls of strawberry shortcake out to the porch. David, Albert, Brendan, Brigit, Barbara, and Aunt Agatha, and Aunt Mame savored every bite. Somehow, the strawberries, shortcake, and cream were the perfect recipe for hope, which everyone felt come alive as they ate each mouthful of Mame's strawberry shortcake. After dessert, the beach kids built a small camp fire in front of the bungalow. As the sun set on the day of the strawberry jubilee, all the beach kids quietly sat in the sand around the fire, missing their friend, Kevin.

*****

Throughout the week, everyone attended to their chores: irrigation pipes to move, potato fields to plow, strawberries to pick and preserve, etc. There was no word from Abigail. The tragedy of losing Kevin O'Connell left his family and friends in shock. A terrible grief hung over the beach and in the hearts of everyone who knew and loved him. On Friday, the terrible dry spell broke with refreshing rain across all of Long Island. Late in the afternoon when the rain stopped, Mame drove Brigit and Barbara up to Baiting Hollow. They knocked on the back door of the bungalow and heard Aunt Agatha say in her lilting voice, "Come in. I'm on the porch."

Mame, Barbara, and Brigit walked through the bungalow to the front porch where Aunt Agatha sat in her white wicker rocking chair just admiring her dear Baiting Hollow. After kisses and hugs, Aunt Mame said, "That was a welcome rain today. The crops really needed a good soaking. David was relieved to have a day he didn't have to move irrigation pipes and spent the afternoon relaxing in his recliner, reading, and enjoying his cigars." She paused and added, "What did the boys do today?"

Aunt Agatha looked out toward Long Island Sound and gestured from the east to the west end of the beach, "They took David's boat out first thing this morning in the rain to explore around the other sides of the cliffs for some sign of Kevin. When they returned around noon, they spread out and combed the beach, cliffs, and marsh on foot. They were here just a few minutes ago. Albert wanted me to tell you to meet him on the third jetty at sunset. That's all he said and then turned and headed out." Aunt Agatha just shrugged her shoulders, raised her eyebrows, smiled, and said, "Come on in, sit down."

Brigit, Barbara, and Mame took their seats on the porch. Mame started talking about the Fourth of July celebration she was planning for Agatha's annual surprise birthday party. Brigit and Barbara stared out the screen windows toward the creek. Barbara noticed that there was a soft wash of pink in the eastern sky which signaled the start of sunset. She whispered to Brigit, "Do you think we should walk over to the jetty now?" Brigit nodded. The two girls excused themselves and walked out the front door, down the steps, and through the sand to the high tide water's edge. There was no one on the beach as far as the eye could see.

As Barbara and Brigit approached the third jetty, Albert called to them and waved them up on the rocks. He was holding a clear blue bottle and a sheet of crinkled paper. Albert motioned for Brigit and Barbara to sit down, so they did. "What's going on?" Barbara asked.

Albert began to talk, "Every day this week and every day since Kevin disappeared we have combed Baiting Hollow for some sign of him. Early this morning in spite of

Patricia Clark Smith.

the rain, Bobby decided to take a walk to the creek once again full of hope that today we would have a word or sign from Kevin. Almost reaching the creek, he looked up along the edge where the sand meets the marsh and saw a magnificent family of five swans, each standing on one leg with their heads buried in their wing feathers, sleeping. He said he paused to admire their stoic beauty. When he told me I was reminded of the Irish myth, "The Children of Lir," which my mother had told us around the bonfire last summer."

Albert started to tell the story: "King Lir had four children whom he loved dearly.

After their mother died, their stepmother who was jealous of her husband's affection for his children tricked them into going on a picnic by the lake. There she cast a spell on them which turned them into swans for nine hundred (900) years. They were to travel through the ice age in their new swan form. Eventually, the four swans landed, as legend tells, near the location where St. Patrick lived. Christianity had come to their dear Ireland. The spell was broken, and they rested there in peace, now nine hundred years old. The children never gave up hope of returning to Ireland."

Patricia Clark Smith.

Albert continued, "Bobby said he noticed something shining in the swan nest and tip-toed up to the nest. He reached into the straw, and grabbed this blue bottle. He brought it with him, and when he met up with me he pulled the cork from the bottle. He let me take the paper out. You won't believe it, but it was a note from Kevin!"

Albert paused and then read the note from Kevin, "Dear friends, I have been captured by the sharks and held by Lord Lahranno in his underwater hideaway. Not sure what he would do to me, I pretended to have amnesia for the past few months. Lord Lahranno seemed pleased to have his son

back with him and treated me fairly well.
Today I am sending this note to alert you
that I am going to try to escape and head
back to Baiting Hollow. Seamus, the old
dolphin castle gardener for Queen Daphnia,
queen of all the dolphins, has been my
greatest confidant. He is going to help me
escape and accompany me back to Baiting
Hollow with Abigail and Daniel. Seamus
said we should arrive during sunset on the
third Saturday in June. Please meet me at
the third jetty on the west end of Baiting
Hollow and keep this a secret among the
beach kids. If Lord Lahranno gets wind of

my escape he will be furious, and I don't know what he is capable of doing."

When Albert finished reading the three beach kids sat in silence. They looked up to see a rainbow arch from north to south around the sunset, paused and watched the sun sink beneath the eastern horizon. "The most beautiful sight you will ever see," Barbara said softly. She then noticed several strange transparent orbs starting to float in the air over the water at the far end of the jetty. She blinked several times in case her eyes were playing tricks on her, pointed to them, and said, "Oh, my, look at that. What are they?"

No one said a word. The three beach kids sat high on the third jetty at sunset staring at the unusual orbs, silently wondering what would happen next. They were startled when Daniel and Seamus leaped, twirled, and slipped back into the dark waters of Long Island Sound without a sound, as if to see if the coast was clear. It was high tide. Slack tide had just begun. The beach kids knew that slack tide only lasted about twenty minutes and whatever was going to happen had to occur during this enchanted twenty minutes. All of a sudden, Abigail leaped out of the water and sat on the enormous blue-black boulder at the end of the jetty followed by Kevin O'Connell sitting at her side. The three beach kids sat up straight with their mouths open wide. Knowing they could not interfere with this enchantment, they remained silent.

The three beach kids watched their friend Kevin turn into his human form. They watched as Kevin and Abigail hugged each other. They watched Abigail, the beautiful mermaid princess, dive and slip into the sound. She emerged after a moment, waved to Kevin, and threw him a kiss. Kevin waved and threw Abigail a kiss too. Abigail was gone. The orbs were gone. Kevin stood up, stretched, turned toward Baiting Hollow, and hopped off the jetty and onto the sandy beach.

Albert, Brigit, and Barbara stood up and jumped off the jetty hollering and waving to their friend, "Kevin! Kevin!"

Kevin looked up at his friends, smiled, and waved. The three beach kids ran down the beach and hugged Kevin. They all fell in a heap on the sand laughing and crying tears of joy. After a few minutes they just lay still leaning on each other and staring up at the stars. Brigit noticed that the tide was heading out and said, "The time of enchantment has passed."

"No," Kevin said softly. "Enchantment really doesn't come and go on the tides."

Brigit's wondering about what Kevin meant was interrupted by Aunt Agatha's call, "Albert, Brigit, Barbara!"

"Mom's calling," Albert said. "We better go back to the bungalow." Albert stood up, wiped the sand from his legs and arms and extended his hand to help Barbara up. While Barbara was wiping the sand off, Albert gave Kevin a hug and said, "It's so good to have you home, Kevin. I'll see you tomorrow." Kevin gave Albert one last pat on his back and nodded. Albert and

Barbara started walking down the beach to the bungalow. Kevin reached down to Brigit, who was still sitting in the sand, took her hand to help her up and asked, "Brigit, I want to go see my parents and sisters and let them know I'm home. Will you ask Aunt Mame and Aunt Agatha if you can meet me back here in a little while? I have so much to tell you."

Arriving back at the jetty Brigit waited for Kevin. She was so glad that her cousin, David, was at the bungalow when she returned and said he'd drive her back to the farm later. (He was always so good to her.) Brigit heard the crunch, crunch of someone

123

walking through the sand near the jetty, turned around, and was happy to see Kevin again. "Let's swim to the raft where we can talk," Kevin suggested and Brigit agreed. She always wore her bathing suit under her clothes for just such an occasion as this. Off came her shorts and sweatshirt, and the two reunited beach kids dove off the jetty and swam to the raft.

Kevin arrived first and jumped up. He extended his hand to Brigit to help her up. They sat shoulder to shoulder staring at their Baiting Hollow glowing in the street lights and moonlight. Millions of stars lit the sky. Kevin took Brigit's hand and began to tell his story.

"My love for Abigail and fierce determination to help her last winter made me ignore Uncle David's and Bobby's advice not to head out in his boat. Blankets of snow kept falling from the heavens. Ten foot waves and a strong current dragged me away from shore until I couldn't see my hand in front of my face."

"Suddenly, my little boat was rammed. I flew out of the boat hitting my head on the side of the boat and falling into the turbulent and icy water. The next thing I remember was waking up in the dark abyss of Lord Lahranno's dungeon. I remembered being taken on a tour of his hide-a-way the last time we visited. Black stone walls surrounded me, seaweed dripped from the walls and low hanging ceiling, and flickers of light darted in and out of the cracks here and there. I pulled myself up and tried to look out through one of the cracks. The dungeon was surrounded by sharks and giant squid. I felt I was doomed."

"I sat down, and my thoughts drifted back to last summer at Queen Daphnia's castle and the angels' lesson on faith, hope, and love. I then knew in my heart of hearts that Abigail, Daniel, the Guardians, Queen Daphnia, you, my family, and all the Baiting Hollow beach people would never rest until I was returned safely home. Then and there, I decided to pretend I had amnesia. I thought that if I was questioned it was better to play dumb."

"Kevin, please stop! It's too horrible to even imagine," Brigit begged.

"Brigit, please let me go on," he urged. She nodded, and Kevin continued. "Sitting in my dungeon cell, I picked up a stick and started to draw on the dirt floor a map of what I could remember of Lord Lahranno's hide-a-way and the waters and current we followed last summer back to Baiting Hollow. A little tap, tap, tap on the outside wall startled me. I stood up, looked out, and saw the old dolphin, Seamus, Queen Daphnia's gardener. When he saw me he smiled and told me not to worry. He told me Abigail and Queen Daphnia had a plan for my escape and warned me not to try to break out on my own."

"Seamus left but came back in what seemed like weeks later. Once again I heard a faint tapping on the cell wall and knew it had to be Seamus. He asked if I was all right and whether I needed anything. It was then I told him I'd like to get a message to the Baiting Hollow beach people. Seamus nodded and left."

"The next day Seamus returned. I heard tap, tap, tap on the cell wall and saw a piece of paper and a pen slip between the cracks and fall onto the floor. I jumped up to see Seamus and thank him. He said to write my note and showed me the beautiful blue corked bottle Abigail gave him to transport my note to Baiting Hollow. He assured me that he'd be back tomorrow to pick up my note."

"I whispered a thank you to my dear friend. When Seamus swam away I sat right down and wrote the note which Bobby later found in the swan's nest. I'm not sure if any of you knew that Seamus gave the note in the bottle to Abigail, and she and Daniel swam to Baiting Hollow and left it with the swans. Abigail knew from the dolphin Guardians that Bobby walked to the creek once or twice a day. He would definitely find it and let Kevin's parents and friends know. They call Bobby, the Guardian of Baiting Hollow."

"Kevin, it seems like the dolphins were really taking care of you," said Brigit.

"It is the only way I endured it, Brigit. They gave me hope," Kevin shook his head, breathed deeply, and continued. "The day of my escape I heard the now familiar tapping on my cell. When I peeked out, I was surprised to see not only Seamus, but also Abigail, Daniel, and the seven Guardians. As soon as Abigail saw me, she held one finger over her mouth gesturing for me to be silent. She then whispered to me that Lord Lahranno and his sharks had gone on a deep sea search to capture other beach kids and bring them back to his hide-a-way. She told me that they had been planning this for a long time. She said that Seamus overheard some of Lord Lahranno's guards talking and let her know. She told me that she went straight to Queen Daphnia with the information, and she insisted that Daniel, Seamus, and the Guardians would help with my escape and trip back to Baiting Hollow. She sent her love, gave her blessing, and waved them off."

"I told Abigail that using the pen Seamus had given me I had rigged a tool to open the simple lock on my cell door. I planned to follow the hallway and stairs of the dungeon and meet them at the rear door of the hide-a-way. Abigail agreed, and the next thing I knew I was in her arms once again. Seamus interrupted and said we didn't have much time. So, off we swam. Abigail and I swam on either side of Daniel with the Guardians in a V-formation following right behind us. It felt as though I was in a dream, so loved and protected. I knew I would be home soon."

"Brigit, there is a message Abigail told me and wanted me to tell you. Abigail said that only time and tide will clarify the truth of her message. Do you remember the angels' message at Queen Daphnia's castle last summer of faith, hope and love?" Kevin asked and waited.

"Of course I remember," Brigit indignantly answered.

"Brigit these three values are at the core of Abigail's message, the one and only answer for mermaids, mermen, and humans to live in peace with each other and our beautiful world. As I sat in my cell day after day, my memory of Baiting Hollow (the sand, grasses, jetties, waters, sunrise, and sunsets) and the love of my family and friends were my companions and my hope. I think I learned a more perfect love for everything in Baiting Hollow when I sat alone in the dark emptiness of my cell. Abigail learned from the angels that this kind of love surpasses all human love. This unconditional love is necessary for us to achieve our destiny, to bring peace and beauty to the world."

"Come on, Kevin. How are we supposed to do that?" Brigit asked, now very confused. "We heard that last summer. Have you done anything to achieve this destiny since then? I know I haven't." Brigit stood up and said, "I'm cold and want to swim to the beach, so I can put on my sweatshirt."

Kevin sighed, nodded, and they both dove in together. Back on shore, Kevin asked Brigit, "Will you do one more thing for me? Will you come with me to this cottage at the head of the third jetty?" Brigit was intrigued, "OK, but why?" Kevin took Brigit's hand and led her through the sand and up the ramp to the deck of a small gray and white bungalow.

"I don't think we should be on their deck," Brigit cautioned.

"Please, trust me, Brigit," Kevin insisted.

Brigit shrugged her shoulders and nodded. She was shocked when Kevin opened the front door to the cottage. She asked, "What are you doing?" Still holding

Brigit's hand, Kevin held the door opened, stepped in, pulled Brigit over the door sill and into the tiny cottage. "Oh my," Brigit whispered in awe. The street lights cast a soft glow within, and Brigit was surprised to see so many treasures from the sea: coral tables, driftwood chairs, a mirror framed in sea glass and silver, bunk beds and cribs on both sides of the room, and a collection of seashells on the window ledges.

Kevin led Brigit to the center of the room and gestured for her to sit down on the sea grass rug, and she did. Her mind reeled imagining what story Kevin had to tell. She looked at him, smiled, and watched him

Patricia Clark Smith.

pace back and forth. Suddenly, he stopped, opened his arms, and announced, "Brigit, welcome to the mer-cottage!"

He could see the perplexed look on Brigit's face, so he sat down and explained. "Abigail has determined that the amount of human activity between the boat launch and the second jetty has made it no longer safe for the passage of merbabies and mermaids. She spoke to Lillian, Queen Mother of all land-living merpeople, and Lillian agreed. Two years ago Lillian talked with Mr. and Mrs. Halls, also merpeople and now farmers in Calverton. Mr. Halls agreed to build this mercottage for the merpeople's safe passage to becoming human and living on land.

Confident that Brigit was listening, Kevin continued. "Abigail also spoke with her friend, Lady Valerie. Abigail brought Valerie to Baiting Hollow as a merbaby when her merparents, Lord and Lady Goodness, were captured by Lord Lahranno. Lillian accepted this merbaby and promised her love and sanctuary. Valerie was adopted by a famous artist couple living in Southampton. Lady Valerie now lives high in the Baiting Hollow cliffs overlooking the sound. Throughout the year she watches the horizon for schools of dolphins. When

Patricia Clark Smith.

she sees the dolphin dance she notifies one of the Twomey sisters and Mr. and Mrs. Halls. If Lillian is here, she will greet Abigail and accept the new merbaby. Lillian then brings the merbaby to the mercottage, and Mrs. Halls takes care of him/her until adoptive parents are found by Valerie. Mr. and Mrs. Halls come to the mercottage every day to see if there is news from Lady Valerie. Valerie's job is to arrange for a family, a home, and a birth certificate for the merbabies."

"Brigit, from now on the mercottage will be our headquarters. The third jetty will be the secret place for Lillian and the Twomey sisters to meet Abigail." Kevin's story was interrupted by David's calling from outside. He had walked to the third jetty to pick up Brigit and take her back to the farm.

"Brigit, Brigit!" David called again. Brigit knew she had to leave and fast. She jumped to her feet and gave Kevin a kiss good-bye.

"I wish I could stay, but I do have to go, Kevin. David is my ride back to the farm tonight," Brigit explained.

Kevin gave Brigit a kiss and said, "I hope you will come back to Baiting Hollow soon."

Patricia Clark Smith.

"I will," she said and ran out the door
and down the sand by the third jetty to
meet David.

******

On the ferry ride home across Long
Island Sound, Brigit stood outside leaning
against the deck railing with her sister
and gazing over the water. Their one week
vacation at the Twomey farm with Aunt
Mame and Uncle David was wonderful.
Visits to Baiting Hollow with Aunt Agatha
and the beach kids were magical. Brigit
would never forget the strawberry jubilee

and would forever be thankful that Kevin O'Connell was safely home.

Within her joyful new memories was the realization that this enchanted childhood world of hers was changing. She remembered Roger's words at the bonfire, "Everything is constantly changing: the tides, the beach, our friends, and our families. And, we, we are only travelers passing by here for a little while."

Brigit reached into her pocket for the wishing stone Kevin gave her last night. It was a small oval and gray stone with two dark blue rings all the way around it. She held onto the little stone, closed her eyes, and wished that the love she felt for her dear Long Island family and friends, the Twomey farm, and her dear Baiting Hollow would always remain the same, and that the mermaids were ok. Then, Brigit threw her wishing stone into Long Island Sound.

******

Brigit started high school in the fall, and Barbara started seventh grade. Sitting in her ninth grade English class, half listening to her teacher go through the expectations for his class, Brigit was distracted by a seagull flying outside the classroom window. She closed her eyes and was sitting on the jetty with Kevin. She wondered what his story about perfect love had to do with anything. She wondered, "If Kevin can realize this, maybe I can too."

Brigit was brought back to attention by her teacher's writing on the blackboard:

"Neither a lofty degree of intelligence, nor imagination, nor both together go to the making of genius. Love... is the soul of genius."-Mozart (Taken from *Soul Provider*, E. Beck)

Patricia Clark Smith.

"Go figure," Brigit mumbled under her breath, "Kevin O'Connell knew that right along."

******